13 MAGPIES

Dedicated to Shaz: thanks for being you and for letting me be me.

The characters and events portrayed in this book are fictitious. Any similarity to real persons, locations or bands, living, dead or any other state of being, is coincidental and not intended by the author.

No part of this book may be reproduced, or stored in a retrieval system, or transmitted in any form or by any means, electronic, mechanical, photocopying, recording, or otherwise, without express written permission of the publisher.

ISBN: 9798874447625

Copyright © 2024 Mark Parsley
All rights reserved

INTRODUCTION

Time is a precious commodity and so I'd like to thank you for spending some of yours reading this book. The stories you are about to read are quirky and I hope that at least a few will have a twist in them that you won't have seen coming.

Each story started with the idea of "What if....." and grew from there. Perhaps if more people asked "What if....?" and then did something different the world would be a different place.

Most of the stories came about during long car journeys, so the M5 and M6 should really get a thank you here (although anyone who has ever been stuck in a traffic jam on either will know that any thanks isn't heartfelt). Four of these stories have been directly inspired by songs (bonus points if you can identify all of them).

Huge thanks must go to Pete K Mally, one of the funniest, most intelligent (even if he thinks a swan is a fish) and inspirational people I know. He inspired me to stop thinking of this book as something I'd do one day and actually write it. Once you've read this, if you want to see how a book of short stories should be written, go and check out his book **Project 49,** you won't regret it.

Thanks also go to all of the artists who continue to inspire me. Whether you use paint, words or music, the world needs art and what you do makes a difference to someone.

Contents

Missing You

The Farm

Lonely

Verity

Blown Away

Shirley

The Romany

Eternity

Motorway Services

Another Night

Heart and Soul

One Man's Luck

Magpie

Second Place

Near Miss

Evergreen Autumn Leaves

<u>Missing You</u>

Standing at the side of the stage, Tony grinned like the proud parent that he was. About to enter the stage from the other side was Mistuiton, the band with his daughter Katy on lead guitar and vocals. This was the pinnacle of the band's career, opening for a huge American band on the first night of their world tour.

This was a tour which would be seen by millions of people and Katy would be stepping out onto the most iconic venues every night and showing the world just how good the band were. Tony thought back to the years he had dedicated to supporting his daughter's dream of being a rock star, and here he was seeing it finally coming true. He couldn't be any more proud.

His thoughts drifted back to the long days and nights driving the band to pubs and clubs to try to build up their following.

The nights of loading their instruments and equipment into the van, driving them to a venue to play in front of a few die hard rock fans. Standing at the merch table and initially trying to sell some T Shirts and copies of their EP to try to recoup some of the petrol costs. Then loading back into the van and driving home whilst the band slept in the back. He'd driven the length and breadth of the country and knew every motorway service station intimately. Soon the size of the venues had grown, as had the crowds.

Then the band broke through onto the festival circuit and the long days became long weekends. Lots of camping in fields, making sure that everything was perfect for their appearance on stage, and always trying to get the band in front of some of the movers and shakers in the music industry.

Tony knew enough people from his time as a session musician but unfortunately he didn't know anyone in a position with influence enough to help give the band a jump start.

Everything that they had achieved had been because of their hard work and determination. And Tony had always been there to support them in any way he could.

He'd got a bank loan to cover the cost of recording their first EP, and fortunately that had made the money back.

Who was he kidding, there was nothing fortunate about it! From the very first time he'd seen the band rehearsing in his garage, he knew they had something special. Katy had been playing a toy guitar before she could walk, and her passion for music just consumed her from then on. Tony had done everything he could to support and nurture that passion. He taught her all he knew about playing the guitar and about the music industry.

She had hung on his every word.

The band's second EP had gone down well and lead to the band growing their following.

More gigs, opening slots at summer festivals, and a lot of scrimping and saving had lead to their first album and critical acclaim within the music press.

Mistuition were on a roll.

And then Tony had had his heart attack. It stopped him from being able to support the band in ways that he had before, but he still went to every gig that they played. Every night the same, standing at the side of the stage, staying out of the way of the bands and their techs, looking out at the ever growing number of faces singing and bouncing along to the music. During this time Katy had written what would become the band's anthem, *Missing You*.

The song got national radio play and even made it into the singles charts, albeit briefly. Every gig now finished with the song, with all the audience singing along and generating a massive wave of emotion.

As Tony was thinking about all of this, the band were working their way through their set, ever professional and looking at home on the big stage as they did in the early days in the pubs and clubs.

He could see just how much the band were enjoying themselves: Steve on drums with a grin wider than anything the Cheshire Cat had ever managed, Phil on bass guitar strutting around the stages with his trademark silk scarves flowing around him and Katy front and centre, singing with raw emotion and playing the Gibson guitar like the virtuoso that she was always destined to be.

He knew that he'd done all that he could and that Katy and the band would continue onwards and upwards.

This would be his last show watching over them.

The chords from the penultimate song faded through the speakers and Katy took the microphone from its stand.

"We've got one more song, guys, and those of you who have seen us before know what it is. For those of you seeing us for the first time, this song is dedicated to my dad, without whom we wouldn't be playing in front of you tonight". Katy replaced the microphone and started the intro into *"Missing You"*.

The haunting melody built into a crescendo and the crowd soaked up every lyric and every note. The band had never played the song so well, and Katy knew that there was something special about this performance. She looked to the side of the stage where her father normally stood. She thought she saw him looking on to the stage but knew it must be a trick of the light.

Tears welled in her eyes as she remembered the promise she had made at his graveside, that she would do him proud on the stage, and deep inside she knew that she had lived up to that promise tonight.

The Farm

Without any doubt, Charlie's favourite thing was lying on the sofa in front the log fire on these cold winter days. A lifetime working on the farm had kept him fit into his older age but he felt the cold in his bones more and more every winter.

As he lay there, listening to the logs crackling in the fireplace, Charlie thought back to all the good times he'd had here on the farm. Like his father and his grandfather before him, he had worked on the mountainside sheep farm. He knew every rock and every bush on those mountainsides and could probably walk all the way around the farm blindfolded. Such amazing scenery and the cleanest air.

He'd never liked the rain which at times crashed into the ground like waves on the beaches he could see in the distance, but had loved trips out with the family to the beach and the sea.

It wasn't getting wet that bothered him, but the rain made his job harder and seemed to make the sheep more belligerent, although no doubt every sheep farmer thought that his animals were hard work in their own way.

As he relaxed on the sofa he could smell the evening meal being cooked in the kitchen. The aroma of a chicken roasting in the oven made his mouth water. The food at the farm was simple fare but that didn't stop it from being tasty and heartwarming. And the gravy that came with his meals just made his taste buds explode with delight. Tonight he knew he'd eat well.

Charlie shifted on the sofa, scratching an itch, and felt his back twinge. The years were catching up with him and he didn't know how many more seasons he'd be able to work on the farm, which troubled him a little. He knew that the farm would keep going, there were plenty of others to continue doing the work, but he doubted that any of them could do it to the standards he maintained.

He looked over at the shelf where all the sheep dog trial rosettes and cups were proudly displayed, and he thought back to all of the competitions that he'd won. The farm had a reputation for producing the finest shepherds and sheepdogs not only in the area but perhaps in the whole country and Charlie was proud of having done his bit to continue that reputation. He'd passed his knowledge on to the youngsters in the same way that it had been passed down to him.

As he reminisced, his mind wandered to the hard times he'd faced. The time that the tourists had brought their dogs to the mountain and scared the sheep, which he and Tom had then worked long into the night to bring back into the field from the mountain. The time when he'd had to kill the fox that had been attacking the chickens at the back of the farm, not liking having to kill an animal but knowing it was what had to be done. The time that Tom had broken his leg and Charlie had stayed with him as he recovered, trying his hardest to comfort him.

Overall the hard times had been few, and the good times had been plentiful, and that made Charlie happy.

Hearing Tom come into the cottage broke Charlie from his reverie and he eased himself off the sofa ready to great his friend.

"Hi Charlie, looks like you've had an easy afternoon", said Tom in a jovial way.

"Time to go for a walk?"

Charlie wagged his tail enthusiastically, deciding there and then that walkies was definitely his favourite thing which brought him the most joy.

Lonely

Julie had never really been that close to her uncle Bill, so when he left the small cottage to her in his Will she was as surprised as anyone. Uncle Bill had died leaving no children and the family had assumed, prior to the will reading, that his estate, as small as it was, would be split between all of his nieces and nephews. But the Will had been short and very precise : "I leave my house and its contents to my niece, Julie Bradley. You're the right person to look after it".

The house itself was a simple place, and obviously hadn't had anything updated or decorated for decades. The one bedroom cottage felt like a time capsule. Julie had expected to find it a mess but was pleasantly surprised to find everything tidy and clean. The bathroom had an avocado green suite in it, no doubt a remnant of the 1970s. The bedroom was sparse: a bed, a chest of drawers and an old wardrobe. All of Bill's clothes were neatly folded or hung in the wardrobe. The living room had an old three piece suite, a table, a chair and an old tv on a unit in one corner.

The kitchen was basic: a few cupboards, an old gas cooker, an old style sink, and in one corner a beige fridge freezer which had no probably been state of the art in 1950. It looked like it weighed a tonne and Julie hoped that it still worked as it looked like it would take several people to move it.

Every room was tidy and clean, and no signs of insect life or decay. Everything looked threadbare and well worn but nothing screamed out that it needed to be replaced immediately, and Julie stood and nodded her approval; this was definitely preferable to her current flat share with three of her work colleagues. She sat at the table and took out the pack of sandwiches which she'd brought with her, not wanting to risk eating anything in a house which had been empty for months. The sandwich was so dry it was unpalatable and she put it back into the box as she walked into the kitchen to look for a bin to throw it in.

As she stood in the kitchen looking around for a bin, she heard a barely audible sigh from the fridge. "Oh great, sounds like that's on its way out", she said to herself. She walked across the kitchen and opened the fridge, slightly confused by the fact that no light came on.

She looked at the wall socket and was even more confused by the fact it was turned off. If it hadn't been the compressor making the sound, what was it? She turned the flashlight on her phone on, got down on the floor and shone it under the fridge, hoping that there wasn't some rodent there waiting to jump out at her. All she saw though was clean lino underneath, with what looked like a small pencil and some torn paper by the far end by the wall, but none of the normal detritus you'd expect to see underneath a kitchen appliance.

Perplexed, she stood up and turned the flashlight off, and heard another sighing noise. "Must just be the pipes or something", she muttered to herself, as much to calm her own nerves as for any other reason. Content she wasn't going to have to catch a rat or clean up some biological waste, she walked into the living room and sat at the table. The next sigh was a lot louder and made Julie jump. There was definitely something under or behind that fridge.

Julie had been brought up by her parents to be practical and pragmatic and so this strange sound intrigued her more than concerned her.

She lacked the imagination to be scared of whatever it could be but instead had a determination to discover its cause.

Perhaps it was a mouse or some other creature which had shot into a hole when she shone the light?
She reached over for the half eaten sandwich, tore off a small chunk and dropped it next to the fridge door, aiming to lure out anything that could be hiding under it.

She stepped back to the chair next to the table and positioned it so that she was far enough away from whatever was there not to frighten it off but still able to clearly see anything which would stick its head out.

She sat still, trying to be as quiet as possible. 5 minutes turned to 10 minutes and nothing happened. Starting to feel a little foolish she stood up, just as a small hand shot out from under the fridge and dragged the bread underneath.

The hand was black and ended in tiny claws. Not a thing of nightmares but not something you see every day either. Julie immediately dropped down to the floor and again shone a light underneath. Nothing. Had she just imagined what she'd seen? As she went to stand up, a small piece of paper fluttered out. She bent to pick it up. Scribbled in what looked like pencil in a childlike scrawl was one word:

Hungry.

Julie turned the paper over and over in her fingers. This wasn't some dream or hallucination, it looked real and the writing smudged on the paper as she rubbed her finger over it. Being pretty certain that mice rarely wrote notes, her level of intrigue exploded. She dropped another couple of piece of bread and cheese on the floor. "Here you go, try that".

Again the hand reached out and scooped the morsels under the fridge. Julie immediately shot down to try to see what was there, but as with her previous attempts, all she saw was the pencil and paper scraps.

She stood up again and went to sit on the chair to try to make some sense of all of this. There was something under that fridge, something that had at least a degree of intelligence but something she couldn't see. Julie had never believed stories of the monster under the bed, but now she was wondering if there might have been something in these stories.

A piece of paper floated out from under the fridge and she stepped forward to pick it up.

Thank you.

Two words scribbled in pencil. At least whatever was there was polite she mused. If it was a monster then it had manners. Julie ripped up the remainder of the sandwich and dropped it on the floor in front of the fridge door.

"All yours, little thing. Hope you like it".

She'd given up trying to see what it was and reconciled her thoughts to accepting that there was something here that seemed benign, even if it was hungry. "Can you speak?" , was answered by silence.

Julie rummaged in her handbag and finally found an old receipt. She looked back at the floor in front of the fridge, unsurprised to see that all of the pieces of sandwich had gone. She pushed the receipt under the fridge.

"How about using that to write on?"

A few seconds passed and the receipt was pushed back out into the open. On it in the same spidery writing was again one word, Friend. She peeked under the fridge just to check, and again saw nothing, no sign of the sandwich nor of her newfound friend.

"Ok, that's a good start. Just hope friend means the same thing to you as it does to me. I've got to go out now but I will be back. I'll bring you something else to eat. Anything you particularly like?".
With this, Julie pushed the receipt back under the fridge and almost immediately it came back, again with one word:

Lonely

"Don't worry I'll come back soon. I guess when Uncle Bill asked me to look after it he was talking about you and not the house. Let's see where this little adventure takes us shall we?"

Another scrap of paper fluttered out from under the fridge. This time there were three words which made Julie smile.

Not lonely now

<u>Verity</u>

We had grown up together, Thomas and Verity, the terrible twosome. Always getting into scrapes and enjoying life as best we could with what little we had between us. She understood me better than anyone and was always there when I needed her.

She was the sensible one, and I was the one who wanted adventure and excitement, and for me the pinnacle of excitement was always playing near the flames. Many nights the flames would attract me, and Verity would make sure I stayed safe. But tonight was different, tonight changed everything.

The evening started as normal, grabbing something to eat, meandering around the local sites, making sure to stay clear of anything likely to get us into trouble. Then I saw it, the flickering light in the distance, a pyre of epic proportions. I had to go and investigate, Verity trying her hardest to persuade me that spending the time looking at the moon was equally as enchanting.

But the pull of the flames was too much, I had to get closer. I could feel the temperature rising the closer I got.

The yellows, reds, and oranges dancing against the coal black night sky, twisting and merging.

Mesmerised I was drawn in, closer and closer. The heat was getting unbearable but still I had to get closer.

With a sudden jolt I was shaken out of my trance, Verity had seen how much I was under the spell of the flames and had bumped into me to break the spell I was under. But in doing so she careered into the flames herself.

I screamed her name, but it was in vain.

The light burned my eyes and I was helpless to do anything. Within seconds the fire had engulfed her, turning her into an inferno, quickly becoming mere embers which floated down to join the ash on the floor, each ember glowing brightly for an instant like glittering stars.

Verity had sacrificed herself to save me, but left me with a pain that I will never be able to leave behind.

"Mummy, mummy look! A moth has just flown into the bonfire. Poor little thing, can we save it?"

"No dear, come away before you hurt yourself. It's gone now, I just hope that other moth doesn't decide to follow it. I really don't understand why they fly so close to the flames"

<u>Blown Away</u>

Sam Argenti stood by the roadside, shivering in the darkness. He looked at his watch, noting that he'd been waiting now for 55 minutes. The witching hour was nearly over, and Sam didn't know how much longer he'd have to wait or even if his intended rendezvous was a waste of time. He paced back and forth, impatient but lacking in any nerves. His battered and well travelled guitar case lay by the side of the road. He knew how good he was, and nothing phased him. Why should it?

Headlights signified a car approaching at speed. The red sports car skidded to a halt in front of him, kicking up a cloud of smoke from the dusty road. The driver's door opened and out stepped a young man with long flowing raven-black hair. Sam looked at the driver and was struck by both how handsome he was but also how young.

 "You're not exactly what I expected", said Sam to the youth.

 "What were you expecting? Red skin, pointy tail, hooves?", chuckled the young man.

"Well you don't exactly look like Satan."

"Ahhh, you were expecting a devil were you? So many people have that assumption", replied the young man.

Sam was momentarily lost for words. He had spent a lot of time finding a shaman to complete the ritual and summon the devil, and yet in front of him was someone who looked more angelic than demonic.

"You summoned me for a musical duel, so here I am. Sorry if my appearance disappoints you", said the young man, continuing to smile as he said it.

"But you're not the devil."

"No, I have had many names but not that one. Some have called me Veles, some Lono, others called me Bragi, Bes, Huehuecóyotl or Apollo. So many names, but not Satan, no."

"So what are you?"

"I am music."

"Sorry? You are music, what does that mean?"

"I have been here since the first men banged sticks to create a rhythm. I have inspired the greatest musicians through the ages. I am music."

Sam was thrown by this answer but then realised that it made sense: he had invoked the essential spirit of music and stupidly assumed that the devil would appear. It seemed to Sam that he had indeed reached the pinnacle he had hoped for.

"So I can't just call you music. What can I call you?"

"Let's go with Apollo. It's as good a name as any I've been called."

"OK, that all makes sense. So if you're not the devil how does this duel work? I assume you want to take my soul if I lose?"

"Oh no, your soul is no use to me. It's quite simple, if you win you get to name your prize, if you lose then I will kill you in whatever way amuses me the most" Sam considered this for a second. This wasn't the conversation he had been preparing for.

"And what does that mean? Will I be beaten to death by clowns?"

"Oh no, the last time I played this game I just went for seeing the poor loser flayed alive. I enjoyed his screams", said Apollo with an unsettling degree of joy in his voice.

Apollo was disappointed to see no reaction from Sam who simply faced him straight on.

"OK, let's do this. And if you want to kill me then so be it".

Sam was not sure if this was now bravado or stupidity. In front of him was the being who had inspired Mozart, Beethoven, Chopin, Bach and all of those musicians whose names were remembered for centuries.

"So what instrument do you want to choose, young Sam?"

Sam was taken aback by the use of his name, but quickly gathered his thoughts. If this was a god, it stood to reason he'd know who had summoned him.

"I'll let you choose first, you are the guest here after all" said Sam with increasing confidence.

"That's brave of you. Let's go classic here, shall we? As you've brought a guitar from the look of things, you can have what's in your case and I'll go with a classic guitar."

In the blink of an eye an immaculate acoustic guitar appeared in his hands, like nothing that Sam had ever seen before. The sunburst wood effect and intricate silverwork and detailing on the frets would put any human luthier to shame.

Sam paused for a moment, a smile on his face. A soft laugh escaped his lips as he moved to the case and opened it. Inside were papers, a bag of mints, a hairbrush, a lighter, a packet of cigarettes, and a small leather case. It may have been a guitar case but there was definitely no guitar inside.

"That was a bit of a big assumption on your part".

Sam laughed again, this time louder, and took out the leather case, opening it to reveal a silver harmonica, which seemed to sparkle in the moonlight.

Apollo looked perplexed, this was definitely not what he was expecting.

"That's different. Let's see if you can keep up"

And with that, Apollo launched into a complex guitar solo, his fingers a blur. As the short piece reached it's crescendo he looked over at Sam and was surprised to see the young man looking nonplussed.

Sam put the harmonica to his mouth and played a perfect rendition of what he had just heard. He turned to Apollo and in a matter of fact tone simply asked "Is that the best you can do?"

Apollo's hands went back to the guitar and he played another piece which would have amazed even the very best of mortal guitarists. Again Sam matched it note for note, playing like a man possessed.

When Sam finished, he fought to catch his breath. After a few seconds he nodded at Apollo.

"That was definitely a challenge. And no doubt you can keep that up until I just run out of breath. So how about you now follow my lead?"

Once again Sam took the harmonica to his mouth, playing a soulful and heart-wrenching melody. As the piece came to an end, Sam held the final note. 10 seconds, 20 seconds, 30 seconds, 40 seconds, 50 seconds. Finally, after a minute which seemed like an eternity, the note faded away.

Apollo sensed victory. He played flawlessly and came to that last note, his fingers digging into the fret board and bending the string for all it was worth. The note finally faded and Apollo looked at Sam with a mixture of hate and disgust. "Let me try that again", he angrily snapped at Sam, who simply shrugged back at him. Again Apollo's fingers worked the guitar strings and again the length of the final note failed to match Sam's.

Apollo visibly dropped his shoulders. He knew he was beaten.

"Well done young man, you've managed what few have ever done. So what do you want as your reward? Fame? Fortune? A solid gold harmonica?"

"None of that thanks", replied Sam. "Just knowing that I've beaten you is enough. If I can beat you then that means I'm good, so now I am going to take this to the world and earn my own fame and fortune. Whatever comes after this will be mine."

He packed his harmonica back into its bag, dropped it into the guitar case. Turning around he saw that he was alone on the road. No car, no guitarist, just the empty dusty road. He picked up his guitar case and turned to walk back home, humming a little melody and smiling to himself. It was a long walk ahead of him and he had a lot to think about.

Shirley

Digging a hole in the garden on a cold and wet April night was not where I wanted to be. The ground was wet, which helped but the number of stones under the surface was making it hard going. I knew the hole had to be of a certain depth to stop any animals digging up the body. I'd only found her lifeless body an hour ago but I was determined for it to be in the house no longer than it had to be.

Finally I was happy that it was deep enough and I dropped the body in. Poor Shirley, this wasn't how I saw things ending for her, but truth be told this wasn't the first body I'd buried like this.

I stood and reflected for a moment, thinking of all of the others. I had to stop doing this, each one I buried made me a little less sad and I didn't want to get to a point where I didn't care anymore. There were too many graves in the garden already. Of course I'd considered other ways of disposing of the bodies but they all lacked the dignity that I think they all deserved.

I thought back to the day I'd picked Shirley up at the local fair. She had caught my eye as I meandered through the various carnival stands. The bright lights and loud music had all melted into the background as I was transfixed by her beauty.

I knew at that point I had to have her. This wasn't a new story; it had been the same before. Janice, Tina, Kylie, Danni, Joan. I definitely had a type and knew how to win them. Each one of them had been beautiful and had a specific look which had captivated me.

They'd all come home with me, and things had always started out well. I'd looked after them, occasionally feeling a little sorry for their confinement but always consoling myself that I treated them as best I could. Some of them lasted longer than others, Tina lasting for nearly a year. That had been a good year, having Tina there to listen to all my problems. Just having some company in the cold, dark house was enough for me though. Since my mother had passed away, God rest her soul, I'd been alone in the house.

I knew I wasn't very good at making friends or talking to people, and picking up a companion at the fair each time it came to town was always something I looked forward to. Having company in the house made it feel more like a home and less like some oppressive prison cell.

A drop of water landing on my face from an overhead tree brought me out of my daydream. I quickly dropped Shirley's body into the hole and began to backfill it.

Living in a quiet neighbourhood has the advantage that there are no nosey neighbours to peer over the fence and ask me what I'm doing, why I'm crying while filling in a hole, or even why I seemed to dig so many holes. I was finally close to finishing so I sprinkled some flower seeds on the bare patch in the ground, patted the soil down and put the spade away in the shed. When the better weather came, hopefully the flowers would help remind me of the good time with Shirley, the same way they did in other parts of the garden with the other bodies I'd buried.

But Shirley has to be the last. I have to break this cycle. I can't be responsible for the death of another one; the guilt is starting to keep me awake at night. And my dreams are not healthy. In them I see Kylie swimming, and then I see her body floating on the surface. I try to save her but she's too far gone. Another body to bury and it was all my fault. I often wake up crying. I miss Kylie.

My mother knew about my obsession but never understood it or encouraged it. I'm not sure if her tolerating me was because she thought it was just a phase I was going through or if her indifference actually made me more determined to carry on. Her approach was just an extension of how she'd brought me up, leaving me to myself most of the time and not interfering.

I never thought I'd had a bad childhood but it was obvious at school that I was not like the other kids. My mother had given me love and affection, in her own way, but I never really had companionship. She had put her foot down on me having a kitten or a puppy, obviously understanding at some level that my basic nature would not have been healthy for it.

Perhaps things would have been different if I'd have had a pet back then. Who knows, it might even have taught me at an early age the value of a life. Things might have been so very different.

The next county fair isn't that far away now, and I am going to have to be strong and not revert to my previous pattern. I'm going to have to stay away, I can't bring home another goldfish just to see it die.

The Romany

The Romany pub had been in the city for as long as anyone could remember. If truth be told, it stood on the multiple foundations of buildings going back to before written records ever existed. There had always been a need for a building like The Romany, and that need had kept the place running. The clientele had sufficient influence which meant that no developer had ever tried to turn the building into a block of flats or a coffee shop. This was a building which served a purpose and met a need.

The outside of the building looked like any other dilapidated city pub. Faded paintwork on the walls, paint peeling from the window frames, the sign above the door showing obvious signs of age. Nothing about the building made it look in any way special, and that meant it worked as the perfect disguise.

It had been under the ownership of Cath's family for generations. Each generation knew how to look after the clientele, how to cater for very specific needs. And this meant that The Romany had very loyal regular customers.

It rarely attracted new customers partly because of its location in the run down part of the city, partly because of the look of the building from the outside and partly because if anyone did step inside, the ambience of the main bar was far from inviting.

The light inside the bar was dull, the interior decoration and all furniture was focused on dark colours. Whilst the optics behind the bar looked well stocked, there was a distinct lack of gaudy colours or promotional items which normally a pub would use to entice people in. In every sense of the word this looked like an old fashioned spit and sawdust pub to any casual observer.

The casual observer probably wouldn't have taken notice of the large black door at the end of the bar, with its finger plate of brass highly polished through centuries of use. The casual observer would never get to see the rooms behind that door. Rooms which all served purposes and met very specific and very private needs.

Cath stood behind the bar polishing glasses. Sitting at either end of the bar were two men nursing their drinks, heads down, staring intently at their drinks. A further couple sat in a booth against a wall. All were obviously regulars, taking a drink before their time came to use the back rooms.

She let a slight smirk cross her lips. This was normal for a Saturday night, and it was how she liked it. Over the years the number of regulars had slowly declined, but those who came still paid her handsomely for her services. Not that she needed the money, she'd provide the services for free.

Previous generations had been well looked after by their clients and Cath was very wealthy if truth be told. However, accepting payment was all part of the contract with her clients.

The contract was a binding agreement, a sacred obligation from both parties to act in a known way. The contracts kept trouble outside the establishment and the inside as a place of sanctuary.

Cath put the glass onto the shelf and reached for another to clean. As she bent down she heard the main door of the bar open and voices she didn't recognise. She stood up with a jerk, not liking what she saw.

Coming through the door was what was clearly a stag party. Six young men, all dressed in fashionable clothing and bedecked in ugly jewellery. These were definitely not the type of people that Cath wanted in her establishment.

The leader of the group strode confidently to the bar. His obvious spray tan offset by his white shirt, muscles underneath rippling. This was someone who took his appearance very seriously, although Cath doubted that all those mucles came without use of some form of drug. That would account for his obvious anger issues.

"Six double vodka and cokes love", he all but shouted.

Cath nodded, and turned towards the optics, glasses lined up below.

"Tonight love, come on. Me and the boys can't wait all night"

As she started to pour the first vodka she turned to face the bar.

"This'll have to be your first and last I'm afraid, we're closing up soon". Cath was eager to get these men out of her bar as quickly and as quietly as possible.

One of the regulars at the bar turned his head to stare at the group. Cath looked over to him "Not tonight Clay".

Whether it was the fact that the man at the bar wasn't used to being told what to do by a woman, whether it was the mix of drink and drugs in his system or whether he had just come out looking for a fight the outcome seemed to be inevitable.

"What are you staring at, freak?"

Cath looked at the man and back to Clay. "Leave it Clay, he doesn't mean anything by it."

"Aw, can't the little saddo talk for himself? Need a woman to stand up for him?"

The tension at the bar became charged with electricity.

Clay pushed his bar stool back and stood up. He snarled at the intruder into his realm. The look on his face said all it should have needed to say: this is my domain, you are not welcome here, walk away or you'll regret it.

The look on Clay's face should have been enough, but some people just don't seem able to take a hint.

"Not now Clay", sighed Cath, although she knew that Clay wasn't listening.

"Ok freak, if its a fight you want, me and the lads will oblige, then we'll come back and have as many drinks as we want."

The group walked back outside, with the large man beckoning Clay to follow.

"Come on chickenshit, let's teach you that lesson quickly."

The big man walked into the night, Clay stood up and walked across the bar floor, following him into the darkness. Cath absentmindedly drank the first vodka she had poured and stacked the remaining glasses back. They weren't going to be needed tonight.

Five minutes later Clay walked back in through the door, up to his stool at the bar, sat down and smoothed out his jacket.

"I suppose I need to go and clean up the mess outside now, do I Clay?"

"Sorry Cath, you know how I get" said Clay apologetically, looking down at the floor in shame.

"It's always the same with you werewolves, bite first and expect someone else to clean up the bodies afterwards."

Eternity

The waves gently lapped against the sand and a faint breeze ruffled the old man's hair as he stood looking out to sea. Just up from the beach, the breeze caused the pine trees to gently sway. If this was to be how it all ended then he didn't think he could have chosen a more peaceful setting.

"So this is where it all ends, is it? I've been waiting a long time for this", said a voice behind the old man. He turned and saw a young man wearing black jeans and a black hooded jacket.

"Not exactly the look I was expecting from you", said the old man, with a slight tone of surprise.

"I have to move with the times, as I'm sure you can appreciate".

"Yes, staying current keeps you in the crowd, and for someone like me that's been the key".

The two men looked at each other for a second and then the old man turned back to face the sea.

He sighed, "This morning is going to have a lot of firsts, but it's also my last. I've grown weary of this world, the running and the hiding. It was always my wish to leave here on my own terms".

"I understand that. It can't have been an easy life"

The old man paused for a second and gathered his thoughts.

"It's for the best, I have done great deeds, for good and for bad. No one would ever understand why I did the things I did. I would just be another monster in a world that is increasingly full of monsters".

"I'm not here to judge you, you know that, right? I'm just here to open the door to the next part of your journey. But I have seen all that you've done, and I think the good outweighs the bad by some way".

The old man didn't reply. It wouldn't be long before the dawn broke and the birds in the trees were starting to wake and herald in another day, unaware of the scene unfolding on the beach below them.

"Do you think a monster can be benevolent? I've killed men, women and children, I've seen cities fall, I've seen so many things. But this is the first time I have heard the dawn chorus. Something so simple yet so beautiful. Should I be sad at how much I missed?"

The young man looked puzzled for the briefest of moments and then stared intently at his companion.

"History will never record your name, you have truly managed to stay anonymous, which for your kind is a miracle in its own way. As for your deeds, well good and bad are just subjective. You killed people and in doing so made the world a better place for some. Ultimately you cannot change your very nature though, and what you did was all that you could do. Your actions should be viewed through the lens of centuries, whilst mortal men filter through years or decades at most."

Both men stood silent for a moment, in the background the dawn chorus growing louder. Finally, the young man broke the silence.

"And now it's time. I don't know what comes next for you, but go on the journey knowing that you could have been a monster feared and loathed by all. Your legacy is not being the monster you could have been".

As the dawn finally broke a casual observer might have seen this brief flash of flame and an arc of light, the sun shining off a scythe blade. That same observer would blink and then only see the faintest of clouds of ash blowing in the wind, as the blackbirds continued to herald in the new day.

Motorway Services

3am in a motorway service station. Not the glamorous location that most music fans think of their idols in. For Tom, this was just part of his life. More time spent on the road in the old truck than playing on stage with his band, the Bathtub Monkeys.

Except tonight felt different. The band had performed an amazing set at The Black Duck to a full venue. They'd played all their crowd favourite songs and it had been one of those nights where everyone had played at their very best. When they'd played their crowd favourite, "Our Rock Guitar Love", it had seemed like everyone in the venue had been singing along with them. It didn't get much better than that.

Tom had come off stage feeling like a rock star, being clapped on the back and hugged by everyone he met. This was the buzz that he lived for.

He remembered the post-show party, being bought more drinks than he could ever remember, struggling to load the gear into the van and then falling asleep in the back of the van, leaving Ian to do the driving. He couldn't remember falling asleep, the drive, nor how he'd got from the van to the door of the service station.

The lights from the building were blindingly bright which Tom just assumed was a side effect from all of the alcohol he'd consumed. Ahead of him, the other two members of the band walked through the automatic door and into the atrium area. Tom followed, half walking and half staggering. His head felt like it was full of cotton wool and all of his senses felt like they had been ramped up.
Had someone spiked his drink, he wondered?

The band took up seats in the fast food area and Tom finally staggered over and joined them. He sat down and stared at his band mates, neither of whom seemed to want to look at him.

"Hey guys, are you all ok? Not sure what was in my beer but I've never felt like this before".

Toni, the band drummer looked absently out of the window into the darkness, tapping her fingers on the table in front of her.

Tap tap tap.

Tap tap tap.

Tap tap tap.

"That was some gig tonight. Ian, you played that bass like your life depended on it, you were absolutely on fire, dude. And Toni, do you actually have any drums left? My god, you both smashed it!", said Tom, trying to get a response from his band mates.

Ian picked up the menu from the table and stared intently at it, leaning his head to one side.

"Come on guys, what's up with you? We've just played out of our skins, best gig ever. And I'm sure there was someone there from that record company who contacted us a couple of weeks ago. Things are looking good, guys".

Still Toni and Ian sat silently, both seemingly lost in their own thoughts.

"Ok, have I done something guys? I know I got a little wasted afterwards but hey, I was on a high" said Tom, desperately trying to find out the root cause of the strange atmosphere.

Finally Ian put down the menu and looked at Tom.

"Tom, this is the end of the road, mate. It's the end of the band. We're finished."

Tom felt like he'd been hit in the chest with a sledge hammer. Where was this coming from? Nothing had prepared him for that statement and it took him a couple of seconds to regain his composure.

"What do you mean, Ian? What the hell are you on about? Toni, what's this idiot talking about?"

Both Ian and Toni looked expressionless. Neither seemed to be angry, sad or trying to hold back a smile. Tom was bewildered and had never seen either of his friends this way before.

"Come on guys, what's this all about? If it's some joke then it's a crap one."

Toni broke her silence. "After tonight, we're not a band any more. You aren't coming with us. Me and Ian have to go on a journey on our own, but you have to stay. Just don't forget us."

Tom's head was spinning. He heard the words that they were speaking but didn't understand why they were saying them. His headache started to throb and he could feel himself struggling for breath.

Both Ian and Toni got up from their chairs and started to walk away from the table.

"Bye Tom, it's been a blast, mate. But this is where we leave you", said Ian as he strode towards the exit.

As Toni walked past Tom, she leant over to him and gently kissed him on the lips. She pulled away and then firmly kissed Tom again on the forehead.

"I should have done that a long time ago. Hopefully this is what you need to keep going on, Tom, don't let this be the end, you'll survive."

And with that, she jogged over to Ian, both of them walking out of the door, neither looking back. The automatic door shut and both were quickly enveloped in the darkness outside.

Tom tried to stand but all the energy had gone out of his body. He was a broken man. He didn't understand what had just happened nor why he felt physically unable to jump up and run after his two friends. Each breath took more and more effort until he finally slumped forward onto the table, slipping into unconsciousness.

"Andy, Andy, this one's still alive!"

The paramedic stopped administering CPR to the young man on the floor now he was convinced that the patient was breathing. The other paramedic by the side of the van looked over to him.

"He's the lucky one out of the three then, these others are beyond help. That van obviously hit the barrier at some speed. Looks like the driver broke his neck on impact and I assume the passenger wasn't wearing a seatbelt. Pity, she looks like a pretty young thing."

The young man on the floor gasped for breath. He turned his head to look over at the van which was wedged into the motorway central barrier, the Bathtub Monkeys logo on the bonnet crumpled beyond recognition.

Despite the pain he felt, he could still feel the warmth of the kiss on his forehead.

Another Night

Another night, another protection duty for Dave. Not that he minded doing his job, quite the opposite in fact. He'd been brought in two years ago by Glenda Le Fay to protect her from things that might do her harm, not that he ever really understood what that meant.

The old lady had built an empire from her Mystic brand: perfumes, clothes, books and films. But with fame came a darker side; overzealous fans and other risks. Whilst Ms Le Fay had the very best in alarms and security that money could buy, Dave brought with him a very special set of skills, and it was those skills that were ready to be deployed ever night, whatever may come.

So tonight, Dave started his normal patrol, walking around the mansion the same way he had done night after night, every night. He started off outside, patrolling the borders of the property, taking note of everything around him.

It had been a hot day and the air was still humid and oppressive.

Everything looked in order but Dave couldn't shake off the feeling that something was wrong.

The hairs on the back of his neck seemed to be charged with electricity.

The feeling stayed with him as he wandered back into the house. He walked through rooms, looking for anything out of place or unexpected, and on his first pass he was happy that nothing was amiss., but he still couldn't shake that feeling.

Time for a sit down in his favourite chair in the study, not thinking about sleep but instead with all of his senses on high alert.

Two years and nothing had interrupted his routine. His charge had been kept safe and he had not had to deal with anything more threatening than the one time a mouse had got into the kitchen, which he'd dealt with before Ms Le Fay had seen it.

As his mind drifted back to the mouse incident, he thought he heard a faint sound in the kitchen. Was this another rodent in the wrong place at the wrong time?

He stood up, and silently moved towards the kitchen, almost invisible in the shadows. As he approached the kitchen the hairs on the back of his neck stood up, as if the electric charge had been turned up in power. He was sure that whatever was causing the sound it was no mouse.

Placing himself in a dark corner in the kitchen, Dave patiently watched the back door, waiting to see just who or what was going to come through. The door slowly opened, the intruder being wary to make the least amount of noise possible.

Dave slowed his breathing and tensed his muscles. He didn't know how the intruder had managed to get past the alarms but that didn't concern him. He was here and he was going to do his job.

He stood and watched, ready to jump into action and engage the intruder, every instinct telling him to wait until the right moment to pounce. Every muscle tense, every sense heightened, he was ready. This was what he had been brought in for, the opportunity he had been waiting his whole life for.

The intruder stepped into the kitchen and for a split second Dave was shocked to see a waif-like child moving through the doorway. In that split second Dave also realised that whilst it may have looked like a child, it definitely wasn't human. Its clothes moved as if part of the being itself and not as material covering a body and there was no tell-tale rustling of cloth. A slightly putrid smell reached his nostrils. And then there were the eyes.

Piercing red, with a glow which no contact lens could ever create.

Any other guard at this point may have shrunk back into the darkness, afraid of being spotted and afraid to engage this other-worldly creature.

But Dave was not just another guard, he had vowed to protect his charge from all harm, and all harm meant whatever should come his way. Tensing all of the muscles in his legs, and taking a deep breath, he sprang forward, hitting the creature dead centre of its chest. Dave may not have been huge in stature but his momentum and the surprise factor all worked to cause the creature to stagger backwards, snarling and hissing as it did so.

"Who are you that dares to strike me?", the creature snarled, showing a mouth full of small sharp fangs.

"Who I am is not important, all you need to know is that you are not wanted here and I will not let you pass".

Adrenaline coursed through Dave's veins, his body honed to be a weapon, his instincts all ready to direct his next move.

The creature stepped forward again, and this time Dave lashed out at it, catching it across the face and causing it to howl in pain. The creature struck back, talons on the end of spindly fingers raking across Dave's ear and across his shoulder.
White hot pain shot through his body momentarily as he pivoted and struck back.

Blow for blow, the fight continued as the two protagonists moved around the kitchen like choreographed ballerinas. Dave could feel blood dripping from multiple wounds but still he fought on. Moving more by instinct and with a muscle memory developed from years of training, he matched the creature's every move.

Finally, with one gargantuan effort he hurled himself at the creature and clawed at its eyes, or where its eyes should have been. A shriek pierced the otherwise silent night as the creature threw its hands to its face.

"My eye, my eye! What have you done, damn you! You were not supposed to be here!", the creature wailed, a dark liquid slowly dripping down its face.

Dave backed away to reassess the situation. At the same time the creature slowly backed towards the still-open door.

"I will be back, this is not the end", hissed the creature, as it continued to back away.

"And I'll be here waiting and ready", replied Dave with a bravado fuelled by adrenaline.

The creature suddenly turned and sped through the door, Dave followed, but by the time he reached the doorway there was nothing to see outside.

The creature's shriek had woken his employer and Dave heard footsteps come down the stairs and the kitchen light was turned on.

"Oh Dave, what has happened? Come here, my darling , and let me look at those wounds."

Dave staggered towards Ms Le Fay, deep scratches on his face and side stinging and causing him to wince as he moved. For now the house was safe, and Dave knew he'd done his job well.

"Good cat, you've earned your keep tonight"

No one ever said being a witch's cat was easy, but Dave would not have it any other way.

Heart and Soul

Rikki Starr sat upright in his hospital bed. Tubes and wires connected him to machines which monitored his vital signs, which an observer would have noticed slowly getting weaker. The room was the best that the private hospital could provide, no expense spared for the final hours of a mega rock star.

Flowers sent from some of his friends tried to mask the smell of disinfectant, but no matter how hard the room tried to disguise it, there was no hiding the fact that this was a hospital.

The door to his room opened and in stepped a beautiful woman, wearing the finest suit available and snakeskin shoes which Rikki wasn't entirely sure were actually shoes at all.

"I've been waiting for you to come. I assume normal visiting hours don't apply to you? It's been a long time, Lou."

The business woman looked out of the window at the night lights from the city, closing the door behind her.

"No, I'm pretty much free to come and go as I please", she replied matter of factly.

"You haven't aged a day since we first met, I'd have hoped you'd have at least a few grey hairs, if nothing else, just to keep up the illusion", said Rikki, remembering back to the day, twenty years ago, when he first walked into the head office of Esyfer Records to sign the deal which would change his life.

"Not that many people get to meet me face to face nowadays, most of my work is outsourced. But for you, I'm making an exception. This is going to be something new, isn't it?"

A look passed over her face which seemed to be a mixture of humour and genuine intrigue. Rikki stared at her, realising that for the first time Lou was encountering a situation where she wasn't in complete control.

Lou adjusted her jacket slightly and composed herself.

"So Rikki, I've stuck by my side of the bargain, and now it's time for you to", said Lou, pausing for effect.

"The only problem is that we don't know what's going to happen next do we? That little wording that you inserted into the contract, which I didn't think anything of at the time. Oh, how naive I was", she finished with a chuckle which to Rikki didn't sound like Lou saw any humour in this situation.

Lou suddenly had a contract in her hands and waved it with an overly dramatic flourish at the stricken figure in the bed.

"Ten little words, which seemed so insignificant at the time, but could now mean everything for you, Rikki. Let's just see if you did really live up to everything in the contract. I've given you health, success, fame, adoration of fans all over the world. And all for that clichéd price of your soul."

Lou paused for effect, or was it that she was in a situation now that she had never experienced before? This scene had played out so many times over the years but this time one small alteration to the contract had introduced a significant degree of uncertainty.

"At the time, Lou, you thought it was cute."

Lou flourished the contract again, but this time ten words glowed with a bright red flare. A younger Rikki would have been amazed at this and wondered how she had managed the trick, but the older Rikki was wiser.

I WILL COMMIT MY HEART AND SOUL TO MY MUSIC

"Yeah, little wannabe rock star who wanted to throw everything into his music to become a global star. Cute. Except you knew it wasn't that simple didn't you? Even specifying that you retain the ownership of your music in perpetuity, very clever", said Lou with a degree of venom in her voice.
It was obvious to Rikki that Lou was not enjoying this situation.

"It was never about the fame and fortune, Lou, it was always about the music. I wanted the fans to fall in love with it, hear the messages, and who knows, even change their lives for the better because of it."

The machines monitoring Rikki's life continued to display decreasing numbers.

Rikki had specified a "Do No Resuscitate" order with the hospital so there would be no alarms or panicked rushing around when the heart beat finally moved to a flat line.

Rikki Starr would be no more, and he was fine with that. This was his first time in a hospital as a patient, and he was going to make sure that his final moments were as tranquil as possible. He had spent a lifetime avoiding drama and his exit from this world would be no different.

"Are there any last words, Rikki? Anything you'd like me to leak to the music press to cement your place in history?", said Lou with a sneer.

"I think I've said everything I need to say in my songs. It's been a wonderful journey, Lou, and strange to think how much good you've done without knowing it", said Rikki, laughing. The laughter soon turned into a deep, rasping, cough.

Lou chuckled, as much to herself as at what Rikki had just said.

"We had some good times, Rikki, but you were never my little prince of darkness that I'd hoped you'd be. No, you may have partied with the best of them but you always seemed to know your limits. If I didn't know better, I'd have thought you had a deal with the other side. But that's not how it works, is it?" said Lou, trying to provoke a reaction from Rikki.

Rikki just smiled and shook his head.

"No, I only had one deal, but it was a deal on my terms and not yours. I always thought you were cleverer than that, but seems not."

For an instant a look of hatred flashed across Lou's face, but in an instant her looks returned to the same beauty that she had maintained for so many years.

Rikki slowly closed his eyes, his breathing becoming more shallow, until a final, imperceptible, gasp left his lips and his heart monitor finally flat-lined. A thin smile remained on his face. A casual observer would have just seen an old man peacefully sleeping.

The heart monitor started to beep and Lou walked around the bed and turned it off. She had not waited all these years for this moment only to be interrupted by some doctor or nurse.

She stood and watched the body on the bed. Normally at this point a single bright light would exit the body, which she would collect. That was the deal. She waited, and finally one small golden light emerged from the body of the now deceased rock star.

She reached over to it but it quickly moved out of her grasp, moving towards the wall and then through it into the night outside. Then another emerged, then another, then ten, then more, until the whole room was filled with small lights resembling a swarm of fireflies. The lights swirled around the body and then started to disperse, flying outwards through the walls, window, floor and ceiling.

Lou stood and watched, in admiration; feelings she had never experienced before. This was definitely a first for her. She may have been beaten but she could at least appreciate her opponent.

"Well done Rikki Starr. You have indeed beaten me. Not many achieve that. It looks like a piece of your soul is going to live on in every song you ever recorded".

The last of the small globes of light had now left the room, flying out into the night. All that was left in the room was the body of a rock star who really had committed everything to his music.

<u>One Man's Luck</u>

Gary sat down on the park bench, taking in the smells and the sounds of the city around him. He'd managed to sneak away from his changing room in the stadium, and with the hood on his jacket up had managed to avoid anyone recognising him, as he'd casually walked out with the last of the crowd.

What a night it had been, playing in front of thirty thousand adoring fans. He still couldn't comprehend just how he'd managed to go from being a busker who played the occasional gig in a pub to being a star on a sold-out stadium tour. Life isn't supposed to be a fairy tale, he told himself, but here I am living one.

Lost in his thoughts, Gary hadn't noticed the old man sit on the bench next to him.

"Are you ok?", the old man asked

Gary was momentarily jolted back into the real world and looked at the man.

"Yeah, I'm fine. More than fine in fact", replied Gary, a thin smile on his lips as he shook his head.

"You don't remember me, do you?", the old man replied.

Gary looked intently at the old man, trying hard to place the face. He'd met so many people over the last 12 months that he'd lost the ability to put names to those faces.

"I'm sorry man, I don't recall you. I've had a long day and a hard night, d my brain is a little fuzzy at the moment" , Gary replied.

"I know, I saw you play tonight. Thought it was very good. But then again I've always thought you were good, and just deserved the right breaks", chuckled the old man.

"Thanks. Sorry, what did you just say?", said Gary, trying hard to recall just who the stranger was. Then it hit him, "I remember now, you're the guy I pulled out of that canal a couple of years ago".

"Yes, its me. Had a few too many celebrating that night and next thing I know I'm in the canal. Never did learn how to swim. You saved my life that night, ruined your shoes doing it, if I remember rightly".

"What's a pair of suede shoes compared to someone's life? They weren't my favourites anyway", Gary laughed

The two men sat quietly, both reflecting on that cold night in Dudley.

"I never did get your name. Even that night you just thanked me and wandered off into the dark", said Gary, breaking the silence.

"I'm Caerus, nice to finally talk to you Gary."

"It's funny, after that night everything just seemed to have gone right for me. You're obviously my good luck omen."

"You could say that", said Caerus, first chuckling then bursting out into hearty laughter.

"What's so funny?", asked Gary, not understanding what had amused the old man so much.

"Oh, just that I always repay my debts, and that was a big debt to repay. In this world it's harder and harder to pay debts back like that sufficiently. You've certainly kept me busy." Again Caerus chuckled.

"I feel like I'm really missing the joke here" replied Gary, starting to get a little annoyed that he didn't understand fully what the old man was telling him. A thought nagged at the back of his mind, but he didn't know how to put it in words.

"There's no joke I promise you. Did you really never think to question all the circumstances that lead you to where you are now?", asked Caerus, a more serious look on his face.

"Ok, I don't know what you're suggesting here. There's probably hundreds of things that happened, I've always thought I was just lucky. I know some things were a little weird and improbable, but haven't really thought about them", lied Gary.

There were plenty of things that had happened in the last two years which at the time had felt like blind luck but he'd recently began to wonder whether they'd been more to them. He believed in coincidences, but there came a point where too many coincidences seemed to suggest something more than blind luck.

Caerus paused for a second.

"Weird and improbable are my style. I'm good at making the right things happen at the right time, well, the right time as I see fit", said Caerus, again amused at his own words.

"Can you please stop talking in riddles? It's been a long day, I'm tired, I'm confused and you're not making any sense", said Gary wearily.

Caerus fixed Gary with an intense stare.

"How ideal was it that the original singer booked for that night at The White Lion was ill, and that you were the only person able to step in at the last minute?", Caerus paused for a second to let his words sink in.

"Or that the A&R guy from ZSMP Records happened to go to the wrong venue that night and saw you play in the White Lion and then took your demo CD?"

Gary sat still, trying to take in all that he was being told and trying to understand just what the old man was suggesting.

Caerus was in full flow now.

"And that mysteriously all of the other CDs in his car wouldn't play, so he had to listen to yours on his drive home? Or that his daughter found the CD in her bedroom , and played it and loved it, and then badgered her father about you? And after that he decided to sign you, and not the other bands he'd been scouting?"

"And let's not forget your first gig as support for that big band, where the fan had an asthma attack, and you jumped down from the stage and helped get security to get her to safety. Can you remember how the media went crazy over that? Do you think all of those things were coincidence or sheer luck?"

Gary tried to take this all in. "So you did all that?", was all he could utter.

Caerus laughed. "Lots of casual breaking and entering, adding some mild toxins to the milk in someone's fridge, breaking into a car and screwing with someone's Sat Nav and also scratching all their CDs. The asthmatic thing , that was just plain luck, I can't claim that one completely, although I did steal her inhaler". His chuckle became a belly laugh.

Gary was dumbstruck. Hearing all this replayed to him in such a matter of fact manner. "So my success has come at a cost to all those other people?"

Caerus paused for a moment. "Yes. Nothing comes for free". His tone had gone from jovial to serious.

This was the reply that Gary had expected but not what he wanted to hear.
"But some of those people are probably so much more talented than I am. It doesn't seem fair."

"No one ever said life is fair. Just be thankful that you got the breaks that you did. If it hadn't been you it would have been someone else. It's just your breaks were a little less arbitrary. And who says those other people are more talented? I just set wheels in motion, you did the rest."

"Oh I am thankful, I just worry about the cost."

Both of them sat on the bench, looking out into the darkness, waiting for the other to say something.

Finally, Caerus broke the silence.

"Balance that cost by passing your good fortune on to others. Play it forward, as the youngsters say. I've given you a headstart, how you use your talent and what you do with it is now all down to you."

And with that, Caerus stood up and started to walk away.

Gary called after the departing figure, "Will I see you again?"

Caerus paused for a second before turning and smiling at Gary.

"I may be around, but I don't think we'll chat again. You're a good person, you'll know what to do in future."

He turned and headed into the night, whistling one of Gary's tunes. Gary had never felt so alone but also so determined to make a difference. He may not be a demi-god but that wouldn't stop him paying his good fortune forward.

Magpie

Writer's block was killing me. I'd never experienced this before and despite trying endless ways to break it, I still found myself sitting in front of my study window staring at the blank page on my laptop screen. Moving to the small house in the middle of nowhere had seemed like a way to help me focus my thoughts, and whilst the view of nature from the window was good for my soul it was doing nothing for my creativity.

"God, I'd do anything to end this drought!", I shouted out to no one.

I started typing, no real focus, just getting something onto the page to fight off the dread that my days as an author were coming to an end. I looked out of the window, searching for some inspiration, some spark, anything. Casting my eye over the stream of consciousness I'd written, I decided it wasn't worth the virtual paper it was written on and hit the delete button. Back to a blank page yet again, the same blank page that had haunted me for weeks.

My mind started to wander, as it had on so many occasions, trying to conjure up at least the initial germ of an idea I could work with. Suddenly the flapping of black wings outside the window brought me out of my reverie. On the windowsill outside stood a magpie, staring back at me.

"Well, you're a striking thing aren't you?"

The magpie cocked its head to one side, as if listening to me. I chuckled. Then I realised the window was open and I had visions of the bird getting inside and causing mayhem.

"Don't think you are coming in here no matter how handsome you are"

I got up to close the window and the magpie hopped along the windowsill away from me, but didn't fly off.
"Caw, caw."
Was this bird trying to communicate with me?

"As you're being so polite, it would be wrong to slam the window in your face".

I reached over to my breakfast plate that was still on my desk, took a bit of bacon rind I'd left, and dropped it out onto the windowsill. The magpie looked the scrap up and down, hopped across to it and after an initial investigative peck, gobbled it down.

"Like that, do you? Stay there and I'll see what I've got in the kitchen".

I stood up and walked into the kitchen to see what other scraps I could find for my new friend, totally forgetting that the window was still open.

I came back into the study with a plate of assorted snacks to see the magpie standing on my laptop. "Be my guest, don't suppose you can do any worse than me at the moment.". The magpie then became a blur, tapping its beak into the keyboard at a furious pace.

"Oi, just be careful, that laptop isn't a toy", I said as I cautiously moved towards the desk, not wanting to alarm the bird. The magpie stopped its furious typing and hopped back through the window.

"Here you go, try some raisins and some peanuts", I said, glad to see that the magpie hadn't damaged the laptop.

After sprinkling the treats onto the windowsill I turned to the laptop and reached for the delete key.

My hand stopped, my breathing stopped, quite possibly my heart stopped. Before me on the screen was not random gibberish:

I have stories to tell, be my voice.
Your well is empty, mine is full of a thousand generations of memories.
Stories which need to be told.
Tell my stories to the world.

I read the words again, and again, and again. I rubbed my eyes, I pinched myself to feel the pain to make sure I wasn't dreaming. No matter what I did, the words persisted on the screen. Words that the magpie had typed.

"You did this? Can you understand me? Am I having some sort of breakdown? Oh dear god, am I really trying to have a conversation with a bird?"

"Caw, caw, caw"

The magpie hopped back in through the window and jumped onto the keyboard, its beak a blur again as it typed. Having finished, it jumped back onto the windowsill, where it carefully unfurled its wings, and flew off into the evening sky.

I looked at the screen again, hoping to see a nonsensical array of characters, because if that happened I'd know this was just some parlour trick or hallucination.

One for sorrow,
Two for joy,
Three for a girl,
Four for a boy,
Five for silver,
Six for gold,
Seven for a secret, never to be told.
Eight for a wish,
Nine for a kiss,
Ten a surprise you should be careful not to miss,
Eleven for health,
Twelve for wealth.

Twelve lines of text, perfect spelling and punctuation. Well this wasn't a parlour trick. And who would teach a magpie to do this anyway? I walked back to the kitchen and poured a large shot of whiskey, gulping it down in one go. Had I finally broken down from the strain? Was I hallucinating? Was this all a dream?

I poured another large shot, and again finished it in one go. I knew the first few lines of what had been written, taught to me by my grandmother many years ago. But from my recollection that rhyme only ever went up to seven. If I was hallucinating then I was calling on knowledge I didn't consciously remember.

The whiskey burned the back of my throat and made me cough, if this was a dream then it was very realistic. I poured another large measure and walked back to the laptop, the words still staring at me from the screen. The logical part of my brain tried to kick in , I ran an antivirus check, as surely this was some elaborate hoax.

The software told me the laptop was clean, and with no internet access here I was running out of ideas as to how this was happening.

Wasn't it Conan Doyle who said that when you have eliminated the impossible, whatever remains, however improbable, must be the truth? Didn't he also say that life is infinitely stranger than anything which the mind of man could invent? If both of these were true then the case for a magpie being able to type became more plausible.

Somehow though I didn't think that Conan Doyle ever had to consider a typing magpie.

I sat down and poured another whiskey, which I slowly sipped this time, trying to formulate some idea, any idea, as to how this could be happening. Every possible scenario ran through my head, and each one being dismissed. I could only come to one conclusion: the bird could type.

Evening had turned into night as I sat there lost in my thoughts and the whiskey was starting to have a soporific effect. The best thing I could do now was to get some sleep and come back to this tomorrow with a fresh head and perhaps find a way to untangle this little mystery.

The next morning I awoke early and wandered into the study. In my semi-drunken state last night I'd left the window open. On the desk was a single black feather, and on the screen, underneath the list of stories was even more text.

The magpie had really been busy in the night, completing six short stories telling of the sorrow of the loss of a loved one, the joy of finding something simple in life to love, a story about a girl finding a new purpose in life, a short story of a boys deepest desire, a story about a rags to riches musicians tale, and finally a story about an unhealthy obsession with gold. Each story was good. No, each story was really good. I couldn't have written better. I read and reread them. This was amazing. The sheer ability of the author to convey feelings convinced me that this was no mere trick, this was something else indeed.

For the life of me, I couldn't begin to comprehend how this was possible, but the words in front of me were ample evidence that some form of miracle was happening in this little shack in the middle of nowhere.

I printed the stories off on my antiquated Epson printer, sat back in my chair and read them again, and again, and again. I could find no fault in them, this was literary gold.

I pondered what to do next. I made some toast and strong coffee and waited for the magpie to come back, Hours ticked by and there was no sign of my feathered friend.

Finally, bored of waiting I went for a small ramble outside, making sure to leave the study window open and laptop on.

As I wandered the local lanes, I felt more at ease than I had in months. I reveled in the birdsong, could smell the wild flowers and faint aroma of pine from the nearby woods. Everything looked brighter and more alive and I felt as if a huge weight had finally been lifted from my shoulders.

When I returned to the house I immediately walked through to the study. My avian author friend had been busy whilst I was away, my laptop screen showing pages and pages of new text.

Three more stories had been completed; the first about a secret in open sight, the next a moving piece about an old man's dying wish and finally a sad tale about a first kiss. Each story was a masterpiece, eloquently written and timeless in their style. Whoever had written them truly understood the human condition, which made me smile considering they seemingly hadn't been written by a human. Perhaps you didn't have to be human to understand what drives us?

"So you prefer to write when I'm not around, do you?", I called out of the still open window.

No response, no wings flapping at the glass, no cawing, nothing. I didn't know whether to be upset at this or relieved.

Panic that my other-worldly goldmine had dried up started to grip me. Had I done something wrong? Quickly I rushed to the kitchen to replenish the small plate of snacks for the bird, placing it carefully on the desk next to the laptop. I wondered if I had offended him by not providing payment for his work.

The evening turned to night as I sat in my chair, taking pleasure in my whiskey and rereading each story. Eventually I fell asleep where I sat, the mixture of exercise, fresh country air and alcohol finally overcoming my determination to stay awake.

When I woke up the next morning my back and neck ached from the uncomfortable position I'd been lying in and my eyes felt like someone had poured sand in to them. For a few minutes I'd completely forgotten about the mysterious new stories and went about my morning ritual. Feeling and looking like a functioning member of society, I made myself a coffee and went back into the study.

My friend had returned in the night and not only eaten all of the food I had left out for him but also completed three more stories: a tale with a cunning twist at the end, another about having a healthy soul and the last about how a simple good deed could create luck and wealth.

All twelve of the stories were now on my laptop. Twelve stories which I was convinced if combined into a book would be a best seller.

Twelve stories which I know I hadn't written but which no one could dispute were mine.

"Caw caw"

The magpie was back on the windowsill, staring at me.

"So you're back? Work here done now, is it? I don't know what you want from me for this, a few peanuts or some biscuit crumbs hardly seems a fair trade."

The bird once more hopped onto the desk and walked up to the laptop. Again his beak was a blur as he typed something new. I leaned towards the screen to see what he had written.

> *There is one more story.*
> *Men of old knew it.*
> *Men have always known it.*
> *Men have always known me.*

"Ok so now you're writing riddles? I thought you only had twelve stories, Mr Magpie. Let me guess, is this last story some great revelation?".

Three days ago if someone had told me I'd be questioning the philosophy or motives of a magpie I'd have called them insane, but here I was, waiting for the bird to type his reply.

The bird just stared at me

The next sound startled me as it wasn't what I was expecting, the sound of my old trusty printer sending out one printed page. The page exited from the printer and fluttered to the floor. I bent to pick it up and read the six simple words:

Thirteen beware it's the devil himself.

Second Place

Joy leaned on the parapet at the top of the multi-storey car park, looking out across the twinkling lights of the city. A gentle breeze swept across her face and brought with it all of the smells of the city, her city. For 30 years she'd lived in the city and knew it intimately. She always knew she'd live here all her life and this is where she'd die. If she was going to end her life then this was as good a place as any.

As she stood taking in the sights and sounds of the city below, her mind wandered aimlessly, remembering little things but not really focusing on anything. Suddenly she was brought out of her reverie by a voice behind her. She turned to see a small man in a camel hair coat and pin striped grey suit. On his wrist hung a large and expensive looking watch and a large gold ring adorned his finger. Despite all his fine clothes and trappings though his eyes looked sunken and gaunt.

"Sorry, were you talking to me? I was lost in my thoughts there a minute", she said to the man.

The man smiled and replied "Sorry if I startled you. I just asked if everything was ok? I wasn't expecting to see anyone up here yet."

Joy thought for a second about how she would reply. Should she just give an inane response and hope the man would leave or should she tell him the truth? For some reason the man's appearance and demeanor set her at ease and going against her natural reaction she decided that there was nothing to lose in being honest.

"No, I'm not ok. In fact I haven't been ok for a long time. Coming up here to look out over the city calms me down, it's like a little island of tranquillity in a sea of chaos and noise. "

The man regarded her for a few seconds, obviously deciding on how to respond.

"Having an island you can swim to when you're in a chaotic sea sounds like a good thing. Hopefully it stops you from drowning. I'm George by the way, nice to meet you. Sorry if I'm destroying your peace."

"Nice to meet you I suppose. My name's Joy, which is highly ironic", replied Joy.

"Why is it ironic? That's a lovely name."

"I'm not exactly the most joyous of people. The world has done a good making sure that the joy in my life is always limited."

George looked at Joy with a quizzical look on his face.

"Limited sounds like a very strange word. That suggests you do have something, just perhaps not enough. Some of us never had anything."

"I suppose. But my life has always been about being second. At school I was always the unused substitute in teams who won things, I always came second in competitions, I even managed to get 5 numbers on the lottery once and won a whole ninety quid. Second is my thing."

Joy could feel the stress coming out in her voice as she unburdened herself. She was sick of always being second, always being the "nearly girl", just for once she wanted to be first. George took a couple of steps forward. He paused and seemed to be choosing his words carefully.

"Sounds like you're not in a good place at the moment. I hope you weren't thinking of doing something you'd regret. At some point the council really do need to put up some fencing up here as a few people have come here to do more than just look at the view."

Joy realised that George knew exactly why she was there, and didn't really know how to respond. In the distance the sound of a police car siren brought her to her senses.

"And what's it to you if I am here to end it all? You look like you're doing well for yourself. I bet you haven't had to live with knowing that you are never quite good enough! Always bloody second! Never first!", Joy shouted back at him, tears starting to well up in her eyes as the emotion overtook her.

"I bet all those people who didn't manage to reach second place would say they have it worse", said George in a calm voice. "Being second can give you the motivation to being better, it can give you something to strive for, something to live for." George paused, hoping that his words would sink in. Joy again didn't know how to respond. On some level she knew that what she was hearing made sense, and inside her head the darkness that had seemed all consuming started to shrink.

"You look like you have plenty of years ahead of you young lady. Plenty of time to do amazing things. Perhaps tonight isn't the night to end things", George said, keeping his voice calm.

The sound of the police siren seemed to be getting closer and Joy looked out to see if she could spot where it was going to. Other than George no one was aware of her being here or what she was going to do, so she didn't think that the police were on their way to stop her.

"Perhaps you're right George, perhaps you're right", replied Joy with a sigh.

"I've always been successful but tonight I realised that my success counted for nothing. My wife died in hospital and there was nothing my money could have done to save her. She was my world, and that all disappeared. So young lady, I know about loss. But do you want to know something funny?", said George with a slight smile on his face.

"Go on", said Joy, intrigued at where this was now going.

"Well tonight Joy you're second again. Except this time being second makes you a winner. Look over the parapet at the road below. Enjoy your life, Joy."

Joy walked up to the parapet and looked down. On the street below she saw a body, contorted and surrounded by blood. As she looked she street was lit up by the flashing blue light from the police car as it pulled up next to the body. The headlights from the car briefly illuminated the body, a man wearing a camel hair jacket, the light briefly bouncing off the large watch on his wrist.

She turned sharply and saw she was alone on the car park roof. She looked around but George was nowhere to be seen, and whilst she didn't want to believe it she knew that it was his body below that the police were now covering.

Perhaps this time being second wasn't so bad.

__Near Miss__

Dan missed June like he'd never missed anyone before. He lay in the grass in the field and thought through how he'd got here. He hadn't had an easy ride in life but he now felt content that he'd come full circle. After today he knew he wouldn't miss June again.

His mind drifted. Back to the war, the things he'd done, and the things he'd seen. He served king and country, he'd done his duty, but it had broken him inside. The final straw had been shooting the boy with the old Kalashnikov who had been waiting to ambush his unit. It was a clean kill, and he had no doubt saved lives that day, but he still remembered the boys face. He saw it in his dreams, and doubted that he would ever forget it.

That was 5 years ago. A medical discharge and a diagnosis of PTSD and some ineffective counseling had followed. Whilst the counseling and therapy had managed to suppress some of his demons the support he had received had not been a silver bullet. Such an ironic turn of phrase.

Dan had spiraled downwards and was at an all time low when he'd met June in the small shop near his house. He had gone in for his daily bottle of vodka, something to help him sleep and to keep away the nightmares. As he'd reached for the last bottle on the shelf he had found himself touching the hand of the young lady also reaching for the bottle.

Most people would have recoiled from Dan, as he looked haggard and unkempt but the young lady had just smiled at him and told him to take the bottle. For some reason Dan had hesitated and instead of taking the bottle and walking to the checkout he'd looked into her eyes and something inside of him melted away. In front of him, Dan saw an angel. Wearing a bright flowery dress and with blonde hair down to her shoulders she was everything that Dan wasn't. They had struck up a conversation where he had introduced himself and learned that her name was June. That small conversation had changed everything.

From that initial meeting the romance had blossomed. With a new focus in life, and someone who he could talk to and who really listened to him, Dan turned his life around. He made an effort with his appearance.

He got a job at a local warehouse which gave him a structure to his week that he'd previously been missing. It wasn't long before June had moved into Dan's house. Life was good, and Dan felt like he was a functioning member of society again. All because of June.

For a couple of years the pair of them had lived in bliss. Dan was attentive to June's needs, and June provided the stability that Dan craved. But cracks started to appear. Dan wasn't comfortable with socialising in large groups and June liked to party with her friends. Whilst Dan tried to enjoy himself at those events it became obvious to both of them that he didn't fit in to her social circle. June had tried all that she could to help him but there were walls inside Dan's head that no amount of love or support could break down.

Eventually June ended up going out with her friends more and more on her own, leaving Dan at home to watch TV, alone with his own thoughts and giving his insecurities a chance to grow again.

Dan thoughts went through all of this, wondering if he could have tried more or what he could have done differently. He thought that if things had stayed as they had been then everything would have been fine, but discovering that June was seeing someone else finally broke him. They had argued, June had left, and Dan was back to being alone.

The spiral downwards for Dan continued until one day he had decided to do something about it. The skills he'd learned in the army served him well and it wasn't long before he had mapped out her current daily routine. She hadn't been hard to follow. He knew June's routine and where she went jogging in the park, and decided that would be the best place to see her and make things right.

He had carefully planned the place which was best to spot June from the best distance to give him time to prepare. Packing only the things he felt were the bare essentials he'd set off early so that he'd be in position in good time. His spot was suitably concealed from casual view so that no one else in the park would see him waiting.

Dan waited patiently and then, five minutes later than he'd anticipated June came into view. His heart started to race, this would be his only chance, and he didn't want to make a mess of things.

Going through his routine of deep breathing he lowered his heart rate and felt calm. Chambering a round into his L96A1 Sniper Rifle he knew that he wouldn't miss June.

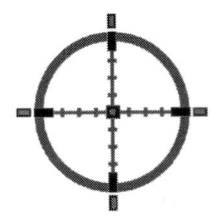

Evergreen Autumn Leaves

The wind rattled the window frames and the rain beat a steady staccato rhythm on the roof of the old shack. Despite its obvious age it had been well built and looked after. Inside the old man sat close to the log fire, lost in a world of memories and thoughts of the past.

The old man was suddenly broken from his reverie by a series of loud knocks on the door. In the 30 years he had used the shack no one had ever disturbed him. The solitude was why he had chosen the location to build the shack there all those years ago; it was far away from civilisation to give him the peace he needed but accessible enough that bringing his work to the shack was possible.

The knocking on the door intensified.

"Ok, ok, I'm coming."

The old man went to the door and opened it. Outside stood a young man, soaked through from the storm, looking dishevelled and distraught.

"Come in, come in young man, you look like you need help and somewhere warm and dry." The young man stepped through the doorway, whatever nerves and apprehension he may have had dispelled by the promise of warmth.

"Thank you, I really appreciate this. I'm really sorry to disturb you but yours is the only shelter I've found for hours and I don't think I'll last the night out there."

"Think nothing of it young man, I don't get visitors here and I wouldn't even leave a dog outside in this weather. What's your name? "

"I'm Steve, and again thank you so much"

"Well Steve, I'm Jeremy, pleased to meet you. Now come in and get closer to that fire. I don't have any dry clothes that will fit you but there are some blankets here, we'll soon have you warm and dry. Let me sort you some tea."

Jeremy turned and walked back towards the fireplace and hung a large black kettle over the fire.

"No modern conveniences here I'm afraid, all very simple stuff, just how I like it. No running water, no power, no phone signals."

Steve took in his surroundings, which were indeed very simple. A basic bed, a sturdy table with 2 chairs, an iron kettle and a cauldron near the fire, what looked like a large butchers block propped against one wall, a couple of large wooden boxes and an assortment of cooking implements hanging from one rafter and two old fashioned oil lanterns from another.

This seemed like the epitome of a backwoods shack from the last century. Along one wall were shelves with cans and mason jars, holding what looked like a collection of preserved fruits, herbs and vegetables. A collection of large knives and cleavers hung at one end of the shack, all of which looked clean but well used. The only thing missing in Steve's mind from making this a clichéd hunter's cabin was the lack of trophies on the wall.

Jeremy pulled one of the chairs closer to the fire, opened a box and brought out a large blanket. "Here, sit here and wrap this around yourself, you'll be warm in no time. So how did you end up at my door?"

Steve paused, there was something that didn't seem quite right about the man's very forthright manner, but he put it down to the old man not being used to company.

"I was hiking before the storm hit, no GPS or phone signal out here. When the storm started I got turned around in the woods and I've been wandering for hours. Then I saw the light from your windows. And here I am. I'm really grateful for your hospitality, really I am"

Jeremy picked up an old cloth, moved to the kettle and poured some steaming water into a teapot.

"Think nothing of it son, just doing the right thing. I mean statistically it's not likely that you're a serial killer", Jeremy chuckled at this as he took down an enamel mug from a hook and poured in some of the contents from the tea pot.

"Here, drink this, it'll warm you through."

Steve took the hot mug and took a sip. It didn't taste like any tea he'd ever had before but wasn't unpleasant. The way he was feeling any hot drink right now was like nectar.

"This is different, don't think I've ever had anything quite like it before. What kind of tea is it?"

"Oh it's just something I've made myself over the years. I've found it to be just the right formula."

Steve could feel himself warming up, and his fingers and toes no longer tingled from the cold. He gulped down the remainder of the warm tea and went to place the mug on the table. As he did so the mug dropped from his hand and he realised that he was losing all sensation in his extremities.

"What was in it, I think I'm having an allergic reaction!"

"Oh no son, it's just the normal effects."

Steve tried to stand but as he did his legs gave way from under him and he crumpled beneath him and he hit the floor with a hard thump. He found himself unable to move his legs or arms, breathing heavily as panic set in.

"Don't worry son, the effects will wear off eventually. It took me a long time to get the strength and mix of the mushrooms just right so that it incapacitates but doesn't stop you breathing. Lots of practice, lots of mistakes. Right, let's prop you up so you're more comfortable."

Jeremy picked Steve up under the armpits showing surprising strength for a seemingly old man. He settled Steve against the frame of the bed and sat back down on his chair.

"Wrong place wrong time I'm afraid son. This was my last season, I can't be digging the holes and carrying the weights like I used to. And my memory isn't what it was. 40 years I've been planting in this forest, and it's all taken its toll. No one has ever been here, no one knows what I've done, and no one would have ever known if you hadn't come along. But as soon as I saw you at the door I knew that my story had one last chapter."

Jeremy adjusted his position in the chair, looking at Steve to make sure that the young man was still conscious.

"These woods have always been a sanctuary for me, I know them better than I know the scars on my hands. I tried living in the town after my parents passed on but it never suited me, too much noise, too many people, too frustrating. I like the peace here. The towns hereabouts have always been good to me, good hunting round here. "

Steve sat and listened to the old man in front of him talking, hoping against hope that the conclusions he had come to weren't going to play out. He was helpless and in a situation you only read about in Stephen King novels.

"It was always hard work, but I enjoyed it. Having the mule used to help, she was a good girl. But she finally passed on in the spring. Had to dig a really big hole for her, got to bury them 6 feet down, stopped the bears from smelling her and digging her up. She deserved her peace. They all deserved their peace."

Jeremy seemed to drift off into his memories for a minute, lost in wherever his thoughts had taken him.
Steve tried to speak but found that whilst he could move his jaw his vocal chords seemed frozen.

"It was always seeing the light leave their eyes that I found addictive. That last gasp, then knowing it was all over. All good things come to an end."

Again Jeremy drifted off into thinking about his past deeds.

"Yes, all good things end. Every apex predator reaches a point where he can't hunt any more and they go off into the woods to die. It's nature's way. No different for me. The doctor said the cancer will kill me soon, so time for me to head out and die how I want to. "

Jeremy paused to catch his breath and broke into a coughing fit. Steve could see that the handkerchief that Jeremy had used was caked in blood, some of which looked fresh. Steve could feel himself getting drowsy and fought to stay awake.

"So young Steve, it looks like you are going to be my storyteller. You're not going to be the last thing I plant, I don't have the energy to do that, and don't think it's what you deserve. "

Steve lapsed in and out of consciousness, and the last thing he saw before darkness overcame him was Jeremy placing some paper on the table before seeing him put on a large coat and walk towards the door.

"Have a good life young man" was the last thing he heard.

What could have been hours or even days later Steve awoke, aware that he had feeling back in his hands and toes. He tried to stand up but realised quickly that he was extremely unsteady and that his head was swimming. He looked around the shack and it was obvious he was the only one there. Sunlight came in through the window and all he could hear from outside was the sound of birds in the trees. At least the storm had subsided.

Slowly the fuzzy feeling in Steve's head started to subside and he soon found his dizziness had gone, allowing him to finally stand up and walk over to the table. On it was an A4 piece of paper, clearly marked on it was the shack and what looked like a route back to town.

All over the map were small x's, each with a name underneath, written with what seemed like a variety of different pens. Steve counted 42 of them. His first thought though was that he had to get back to town. Whilst he was still feeling unsure on his feet the overwhelming feeling was to get as far away from this place as he could and back to civilisation.

Before leaving the shack he briefly searched through it, looking for anything he could take which might be of use. In a small wooden box under the bed he found a collection of credit cards and drivers licenses, all with different names.

If he had doubts before that Jeremy was indeed a serial killer then this find removed all doubt, this was obviously Jeremy's trophy collection.

So many different names, Steve could hardly comprehend what he was seeing. All of the faces on the driving licenses, young and old, men and women. Slowly, a plan started to form in his mind: this was an opportunity too good to miss.

Using the map and his compass Steve eventually made it back to the town, the same one he'd parked his rental car in before starting his fateful hike. As he approached his car he thoroughly checked that no one was following him and that there wasn't anyone observing him.

Content that he was alone we walked to the car, looked around once more, and then opened the boot of the car.

The body was still there, wrapped in the tarpaulin as he had left it. This wasn't what he had originally planned but it gave him an opportunity he could never have hoped for : he could bury the body in the woods and when it was discovered, another serial killer would take the blame for the murder. What were the odds of there being two serial killers in the same woods?

Acknowledgements

Thanks go to the following for their contribution to this book:

The bands "Black Lakes", "Raveneye", "Dead Man's Whiskey" and "These Wicked Rivers" for the inspiration that their songs provided.

Sam Spranger and Nick Peck from "The Bad Day" for answering my questions and providing the inspiration for Blown Away.

Andrea Robinson for her invaluable proof reading and suggestions on improving some of the stories, and for teaching me some things about how to write! 183 commas in this book belong to Andrea, as do a lot of the other punctuation marks.

Pete K Mally for his support and motivation

Printed in Poland
by Amazon Fulfillment
Poland Sp. z o.o., Wrocław